Louis James Block

Exile

A Dramatic Episode

Louis James Block

Exile
A Dramatic Episode

ISBN/EAN: 9783337342487

Printed in Europe, USA, Canada, Australia, Japan

Cover: Foto ©Andreas Hilbeck / pixelio.de

More available books at **www.hansebooks.com**

EXILE

A DRAMATIC EPISODE

BY

LEWIS J. BLOCK

ST. LOUIS

G. I. JONES AND COMPANY

1880

TO

HORACE H. MORGAN.

DRAMATIS PERSONÆ.

THE STRANGER.

FATHER.

MOTHER.

IDA.
ALFRED. } Two children.

Scene: *The shore and waters of an inlet of the sea.*

EXILE.

I.

THE STRANGER (*alone*).

Is there in the deed-world a deed, a way,
Worth doing or worth following? Is there aught
That can call out from spirit's secret deeps
The hopes, the longings, that lie sleeping there
Until the hour, the time, ordained of God,
Touches them with light point of spear or dart,
And they leap forth in light? I cannot deem so.
The largest deeds of men are slender waves
Upon the sea's unmeasured stretch; a king
Sits high enthroned, and dim forgetfulness
Clothes him as with a robe; great love of men
Would set the crooked straight, and stem the stream

That flows to gulfs of death and shame, and turn

Its speed to where the happy fields are green,

But age on age the self-same tasks survive,

The work is still to do. So large man's soul,

That all the outer world is but a star

Upon its sky, and from its own deep might

Star after star appears — white lustrous births

From its unresting motions. All things are small,

All deeds but limited by things or deeds;

The sense of utter power, and might unswerved

From its clear end, resides not in the realm

Where souls appulse gainst souls, and the lame act

Halts far behind the wish; in thought alone

Is perfect freedom; even the seeming laws

Wherein all thought is bound, that wizard keen

Unmakes, and from the wide upheaval rears

Such domes as suit its myriad caprice.

The bitter code of good and ill, the feud

Wherein all pleasure dies, the rigorous choice

Compelling men to one strait way, — wherefore

Should the unconquered soul submit its head

To wear the yoke? In sooth there are two worlds ;

I care not for that slavish bounded realm

Where there is work to do, and men meet men,

And strongest cords of relative despair

Encircle you; I see no cause to act;

I cast mine eyes upon the course of years

Even to the pale beginning. I see the world

Much like itself, bent double on its deeds,

And seeking the impossible, — to make

The world of work reflect the world of thought.

It is in vain, a futile opposition

To the essential framework of the world;

There are two worlds, a contrast sharp and dire,

And reconcilement cannot be. I, therefore,

Leave effort proved forerunner of defeat,

And with my thought am satisfied. I see

At will all splendor take on form and hue,

A pageantry of dreams pass through my soul,

Make joy for me past what the things can give;

For fantasy is more than all the world.

It is with thought that I am fallen in love;

EXILE.

I hate the sickly kissings, clasping hands,

The bitter bonds of love that lures us, love

As in the world misnamed, say, rather, lust

Or some such strain which is for beasts, not men.

But lo! I penetrate all mysteries,

I hold the keys, I watch how in my thought

Idea shapes idea, and the sphere

Rounds itself in the mighty thought of God.

I ponder the dark riddles of the sages,

I muse with the sweet poets, I forsake

The chill embrace of earth; — and this is best.

I shall withdraw me more and more, and reach

The peace which mystic faith has dreamed on, peace

Past understanding save to those strong souls

Who can renounce whatso the outer brings,

And live alone that hid internal life,

Which is the all in all, both each and all,

Oneness eterne o'erruling vast diverse,

Intellect pure in pure activity.

II.

ALFRED.

I wish I were at home; I hate the sea,
Where all day long you see no boys, and sand
Is all you have to play in.

IDA.

But you like to swim,
And go out in the boat, and once you went.
With father in a yacht, and stayed all night,
And caught great loads of fish.

ALFRED.

Ah, yes — I'd be
Down in the town where all the men are gone,
And I'd have boys to go with, but out here
You only see the water — just nought to me —

And gather pebbles girl-like on the beach,

And swim but once a day — a mere half hour —

And then we have no boat, and mother calls

Me back if I go out alone.

                        IDA.

                        Strange talk;

I like to watch the waves roll far away,

And how the wind makes them look dark, and how

The little clean slim fish shoot here and there,

And the bright ripples break upon the shore.

                    ALFRED.

But you're a girl, and girls may like such things,

Where I can see no fun.   I never know

What makes you glad, except you want me by,

And often kiss me out of time.

                        IDA.

                        Oh — oh —

You boys have no conceit.   I think it's time
For me to go back home.

ALFRED.

                    No, no, you must not,
And leave me here alone.   We can but talk,
There's nothing else to do, and how can I,
How can I talk with my mere self ?

IDA.

                    Right well;
I sat the other day out in the wood
Alone for two long hours, and all the time
I talked with persons that seemed in my mind,
And they were beautiful.

ALFRED.

                    You mean you thought;
You make my head ache like the schoolmaster,
Who tells us we must think, and so be good;

But I am sure he never thinks, or he
Would hardly scold the wrong boy as he does.

IDA.

You are right dull; it was not thought at all,
It was not like addition, but a dream
Such as you have at night save that you wake.

ALFRED.

And will you tell me what your dream was like?
I little understand you when you speak,
And say these curious things, but still I like it,
And my head sounds as though a bee shut up
Sang in my brain, and I knew what it said.

IDA.

But you must not break in and laugh;
That makes me cry; I love what my dreams show,
And you are cruel like most boys.

ALFRED.

Nay, cease;

You know I never laugh at you; I laugh

Because the story makes me, and you cry

When most I love you; for somehow you seem

Right good when you go on and talk.

IDA.

Well, then,

I will begin. You know the wood I mean —

You cross the hill, and in the hollow there

The trees stand thickest, and all is so still,

You only hear the waters washing faint

And far away. The roses there grow wild,

And in one spot the thick, wild grape-vines grow,

And the sweet odorous roses climb high up,

And you can sit within a summer-house

The good God made.

ALFRED.

I know the very place;

Where we went picnicking, and father said,
If he had money, he would buy the ground,
And build.

IDA.

    I sat there for awhile and sang,
And then I know not how, but this I saw —⁻
The long green grasses swayed, and rose, and swayed,
And all the wild flowers I could see; I knew
That there was little wind, for the tall aspen
Scarce showed the silver of its trembling leaves.
So I grew still, and watched what I could see.

ALFRED.

And what was that? You take so long to tell
What I should say in half the time.

IDA.

       At last
Out from the spires of grass, and all the flowers,
I cannot tell you how, a fairy leapt,

And soon the air was changed, a golden gloam

Came in its stead, and on their swiftest wings

They flew where was a level spot — just where

The mossy old stump stands. I saw them plain,

The fairies of the grass were long slim things,

With queer peaked faces, and long golden wings

They folded round them like a dress of light,

And when they sang, you heard a small soft sound

That was right sharp in sweetness; but the roses —

From them there came small lady-like sweet forms

That were all fire, — but not the fire that burns —

A rosy gentle flame; they flew in curves,

And sang a song that makes me love you better;

But the buttercups would have been joy to you,

For they were stout, and clothed in shining gold,

And seemed to lord it everywhere so that

The violets, so thin you hardly saw them,

Nor knew them from the air, scampered away

When the gold tyrants came; but night would come

Before I told you all.

ALFRED.

What did they there?

IDA.

I cannot tell; I heard their voices small,

And they flew here and there that — as, at night

When you put head beneath the coverlet,

You see the fire and color interweave —

Their forms of many hues blended and mixed

And fell apart, a shifting play of flames,

Red, blue, and gold, and all so full of glee

That now my heart is glad to think upon it.

I sat right still, and tried to stop my breath,

Till I began to weep, and then I laughed, —

And at the sound, they vanished, one and all.

ALFRED.

That is a pretty tale; you must have slept

And dreamed.

IDA.

If you go on as you do often,
I shall be sorry that I told you.

ALFRED.

You say
You saw, and were awake? Hard to believe;
Why do I never have such luck as you?
But then I often find things when I walk,
And you find nothing.

IDA.

Well, then, be content.

ALFRED.

But do you think the fairies really are,
And live within the grass and every flower?
Why then they die whenever flowers are plucked;
You cannot make me think that such things are,
I never saw one, and you only dreamed.

2

IDA.

You are too hard; why do you make me speak,
And tell you things, if you will treat me so?

ALFRED.

There, now, you cry, and yet I meant no harm.
Come, let me kiss you on your forehead white;
Ah, you smile through your tears.   I understand
So little how you girls are made or think;
I saw you watch the other day awhile
The blood-red splashes left upon the sea
When the great sun went down; but father came
And brought the marbles, so I turned away;
But you and mother sat till the dull gray
Came on the sky, and the big ball of fire
Was gone, and you refused to play.   Now say
What did you see?

IDA.

Oh, you must look right hard;

The little waves seemed all to clap their hands

As a red ray went through them, and the clouds

Floated and swept to bathe them in the glow

As they would like to die on the sun's breast;

And he shed forth the light as he would give

All that he had to make them glad, as I

Would do for you when you are kind to me.

ALFRED.

Well, may be I shall know when I am grown.

Now let us walk down to the beach, and play.

I'll build a house, and be an architect,

And you shall order how you want it, come.

IDA.

But I shall want a castle old with towers

All clad with dark-green ivy-leaves, and windows

With small, diamond panes, and a chapel grave

Where I can go alone, and softly pray.

ALFRED.

That is no use; you shall receive from me
A noble gift, — a lofty brown-stone front,
With basement for the servants, and within
The walls well-painted, and with mirrors tall
In parlor; nobody cares for castles now.

IDA.

It shall be as you wish; but see the waves,
How little sparks of silver fire bestud them,
And from the oars the fiery water falls,
And far away the distant blue shore lies
Like an unmoving mist.

ALFRED.

                        Nay, come and play
Here is the sand that reaches up the hill,
And we can build our houses as we list.
Nay, come and play, — what are you gazing on?

IDA.

It is the tall white stranger we saw before,

The silent man of somber mien and garb,

With large, dark eyes that seemed to wish to weep,

And face white as mamma's sweet hand. You know

He stopped and watched us while we were at play,

Nor said a word, but seemed somehow so sad

That I felt I should like to speak, but then

He was so still and cold, I shook for fear.

ALFRED.

Ah, do not mind; he will not trouble us,

And if he does, I'll nit him with this stone,

And we'll run straight for home, for it is time,

If we shall get our dinner waiting for us.

III.

THE STRANGER.

It cannot be; I dare not mar with change

The calm seclusion of my life, — the still

Unbroken sweep of waters guarding it.

My life has all the magical repose

Of some sweet island in a pale lagoon;

The ripples break upon the clear green waters,

The mainland lies afar enwrapped in mists,

The air is of a soft, mixed hue, not bright

As where the beast conglomerate, mankind,

The many-headed life that is but one,

Each puddled with the soul of each, doth dwell;

Even the sun veils here his rigorous splendors,

And paces with slower step the blue stretched heavens;

The woods are peopled but with cool-eyed blooms

And slender well-poised ferns; and here and there

The white fire of the sudden springs, and birds

Whose voices are the sounds interfluous thoughts

Subtly project when several merge in one,

Conjoining rays in concord of one flame,

And the long grasses swaying in the wind.

Here all is peace and intellectual calm;

A mild self-centred spot which needs no commerce

With outward and debasing elements

To make its joyance; here I make my home

And meditate the boundless universe.

I see unfold the endless leaves of thought,

The petals rather of the great world-rose,

Until the inmost heart lies bare; I see

Within the multitudinous blood-red folds

The pigmy tribes of men; and History

Is as a silly tale told by the fireside

When the late night flares in last burst of gladness,

And soon deep rest shall hold the house; I see

The currents of the sap pass down and up,

The ceaseless potence of ideas great

That build and break, and at the hidden root

Great God himself, from whom all comes, who is
And is not the vast flower, and I am He
And All, when I ascend these easy heights.
But nothing foreign may intrude; disturb
The ambient atmosphere with sullen clouds
Born of the breath of unrespective soul,
And the high bliss is dead; disturb with check
Of contradiction thought's unswerving flow,
And the bemired brown flood reflects no more
The picture of the sky.   Here is my fear;
Into pure Contemplation's mystic round
I may not introduce the passions' whirl,
And that strange sentiment the fool man calls
Love; different by a world's wide interspace
From Love as known in Thought's dear Heaven.   I pause;
Yet Beauty is this still realm's proper garb,
The robe external that expresses it,
And, while concealing, bares its secret heart;
And she — the lovely child — would be fit sign
Of its unbroken rest and splendid joy.
I cannot tell how she possesses me,

How my conception spheres her changing form,

As the round sky the centred earth: she flits

Into my every thought: her sweet smiles light

My deepest plunge of search; and science stern

Grows easy, and with prodigal outpour

Endows me with its secrets for her sake.

It cannot be that in my life's clear song

Her footsteps should make discord, or her voice

Not emphasize the surely-uttered words

That are the very truth of truth in forms

That are itself externalized. And yet —

Ah me — I fear lest I, precipitate

And led by sudden veer of impulse, throw

A hasty stone into my placid life,

And harm my safe release from human cares

With rippled thrills of feeling whose far end

Mine eyes discern not nor my thought. I pause;

When first I saw the grave small face, the eyes .

Quite sad, but clear with some internal flame,

The lips closed in an ecstasy of dream,

I felt her as a sure inhabitant

Of those ideal plains where is Thought's home,

Or those miraculous vales high Fancy holds,

The varying image of the things that are.

Nay, I will not give way to fear; I dare

This deed, and quail not at the consequence.

She shall go with me; I will bear her home,

Engird her with most subtle influences,

And she will grow the white rose of the world,

The fairest lady in the worshipping lands,

A priestess in the virgin fane of Thought,

Iphigenia of these latter times,

The marvel of the ages, womanhood's queen,

Untouched of love or aught that can defile,

The lyre tuned to the planet's revolutions,

Star-taught to music, played upon by winds,

And voicing ocean's ancient mysteries.

Yea, I will go, and ask her of her friends, —

They dare not say me nay, I am sure fate —

And if I must, my wealth shall make me way,

For in the world of men I needs must use

Men's implements, although my heart abhors

Contact with these most foul necessities.

Yea, she shall be to me my shaped expectance,

My life made clear to sight, thought clothed in form,

The apex of the pyramidal loveliness,

Like flame upclimbing skywards, which is my life.

I dare the high attempt, and add the gem

Which rounds the ring, past outer might to break,

Wherein I breathe, clasped hand in hand with God!

IV.

ALFRED.

You do not build — what are you thinking of?

IDA.

I watch you, and it gives me more delight,
For I have no great skill of hand, and still
My walls and windows fall as fast as risen.

ALFRED.

This is your house, — four stories high, at least,
With rounded windows, — say how it pleases you;
See, I can make queer figures round the windows
And over the wide door — now, that looks right;
It shall be quite a palace when 'tis done.

IDA.

How do you make it all secure?

ALFRED.

I know not;

It stands just of itself, I think. Here are

Broad steps in front, and basement windows here;

I soon shall finish, and then give it you

In a long speech.

IDA.

And I shall make reply,

And be all smiles, and say it is too much,

And nothing I have done deserves return,

And bow, and seem ashamed till all are gone,

When I can clap my hands and be plain glad.

ALFRED.

That will be fun — you girls are smart in speech;

I think you must have longer tongues than boys,

And pointed ones, for you are sharp at times,

And say what we can find no answer for.

How do you think a story more would look?

IDA.

Take care, or your frail sand-built house will fall;
You always go beyond the safety point,
And are impatient when your labors fail.

ALFRED.

Yet I will try, and you shall sing the song
Mamma has taught you since we saw this place:
For somehow I can build best as you sing,
And raise my walls in concord with the sound,
For music is the only thing I know
Of the strange pranks you often tell me of
As passing in your brain not like my own.

IDA (*sings*).

I hear the waters call
    Unto me ;
Into a dream I fall
    Of the sea ;
I am borne in a slender boat
To where the moonset pallors float.

The white stars in the sky
Glint and gleam ;
I hear no voice nor cry,
Save the stream
That is bearing me swiftly afar
Past earth's remotest bound and bar.

The moon rests on the sea,
Silver white,
And shines in strangest glee,
Subtly bright ;
I pass to the viewless line
Where moon and tranced sea combine.

I am the Lady Moon,
And the sea,
I am the dim-toned tune —
Utterly —
The waves and the flakes of light
Making send down the blue-roofed night.

I die into a dream
Lighted dim,
I am the fitful stream
Of the hymn

The Sea and the Moon and the Night
Fashion for joy and pure delight.

ALFRED.

There now, 'tis done; did you bring down a doll?
She should walk in in splendid state.

IDA.

I know not;

Here is the little one you do not like.
You will not have her mount your marble steps?

ALFRED.

No; but you said you meant to throw her by,
Or give her to the girl lives next to us.

IDA.

And so I do; but I forgot last time
I saw her, and I left the homely doll
In this small apron-pocket unawares.

ALFRED.

It does not matter. Now I think of it,
I'll try to build a church with lofty spires,
And pointed windows, like the one we saw
In the great city — made as though the stone
Into fine lace-work everywhere were carved.

IDA.

And I will go sit by the silvered strand,
And think how each small boat bears thought of me;
For I will give to everyone a dream
That it will bear, and I shall seem to float
Out where the great waves toss and writhe, and winds
Have room to flutter out their widest skirts,
And freely tread the water's rippled floor.
I only would it were the wondrous night,
Set thick with stars, and overruled
By the sweet lady moon.

ALFRED.

Nay, you must stay;

I cannot build alone, for if you sit,

And look on while I work, I can do better,

And my walls surelier rise. Now if you try,

You can make buildings too, old castles quaint,

With rounded peakéd towers, or chapels small

For ladies grave to pray in.

IDA.

It is in vain;

My hands pull down, I cannot raise a wall.

But, ah, the stranger comes — shall we run home,

Or go on with our play and mind him not?

ALFRED.

Nay, let him come, he will not look nor speak.

THE STRANGER.

There is she now at play; her sweet grave face

Not lighted by a smile, and her dear eyes

Abashed beneath the flower-like lids. The sun

Is glad to play with her gold hair, and make

A fluctuant aureole about her head.

Ah, how I joy to see her little hands

Flicker across the sand in white fair gleams,

And all her motions glad as grace itself.

The lips are parted and I hear low sounds —

No song — but some dear chaos of dim tones

That will in time take shape, and be a tune

Taught by God's angels: ah, sweet child, mine own,

It cannot be that aught save loveliness

Can bloom or be where thou art — beauty's soul,

And Heaven grown visible. I have no fear,

I will go speak to her, although the boy

Perforce must bring the world into our speech,

And gloom across our realm of poetry,

Even as a mountain throws large shadows down

Where the small waves imprisoning fiery gold

Weave on the sea the miracle of the song

The day and wind and waters hold soul-hid,

Or as a steep and blossomless review

Frowns with deep shade upon a valley-poem,

Where the mild violets hide in pallid grass,

Where the white foam of rivulets blooms to die,

And all the winds are sweet with endless spring.

Ida.

Oh, brother, he is coming — let us go;

I fear that he will speak, and my heart beats

And chokes my breath.   I feel afraid and strange,

I think his voice will be a wizard spell

To make me do what I desire not — come!

We shall return — nay, come — I dare not move

Save you are by to help.

Alfred.

                    A little while

And we must start — for you know dinner waits;

Meanwhile I purpose finishing my church.

You are just foolish — let him say his say —

We need not answer, and he will pass on.

I am not troubled.

IDA.

Nay, but he will speak,
And his voice cold as are his far-off eyes,
And his words strange as are his pale calm lips
Make me afraid or ere I hear. I know
His deeds and speech will be as fair as friendship,
Yet I would rather pass him by.

THE STRANGER.

A house —
And nearly reared a stately church — dear boy,
Your hands are skilful past the common wont.
Where learned you this fair craft? Your sister here
Gives help with her sweet smile — she labors not —
Or speaks encouragement with subtle words
You are most glad to hear. Were I at home
I might be aid in your exploits of art.

ALFRED.

I care not for your aid.

THE STRANGER.

Nay, if you knew —
For I have books wherein tall dwellings stand,
Made in times past, and wonderful to see,
White temples shining in the midnoon sun
On heights that overlook the fair green fields,
Old palaces made splendid for great kings,
And ivy-clothéd ruins, hoar and quaint.

ALFRED.

I care not for old books, and reading hard
For wits like mine to understand.

THE STRANGER.

His rudeness
Might make me pause — my voice clings to my throat,
And all my body shakes — 'tis always so
When I adventure in the outer world,
Nor dwell secure my soul within. Too late:
I cannot now refrain who see her face,

White and lustrous as the one star of eve.

'Tis not my wish that you should read my book —
These are fine pictures fit for eyes like yours
Or your sweet sister's. If I brought my book
Would you look on it with me?

IDA.

No.

ALFRED.

I think
My sister wishes not to speak with you;
For you are strange, and not like men we know.

THE STRANGER.

Ah, but I have desire to hear her voice.
She is not unlike a dear girl of mine
About her age, and slender-shaped as she
Whom I saw placed in the cold, rain-wet grave,
And I was left to weep. Dear gold-haired child,

How would it please to come with me, — my home

Is in the far-off hills; it stands alone

In a vast garden, where the largest flowers

Blossom and burn the summer through, and winds

Blow languid with the weight of perfumes, where

Under deep trees the winding pathways lead

To lakes set like clear stars on the green sky

Of grassy miles, where in the solemn shades

Of old oak-woods the hours are filled with dreams,

And if you shut the outer sense you hear

The music that is played in fairyland.

How would you like to go, and be mine own,

A daughter in my house of golden spells,

Where all you wished would speed from out your soul,

Swift changed to flowers for you to hold in hand,

Where you should be a queen — what say you, child?

IDA.

O brother, it is time; I shake for fear —

He means to take me with him — give your hand.

ALFRED.

And I shall find a stone to throw at him;
But then he talks like you, my brain turns round
With wondering what he means.

THE STRANGER.

                                    You are not going?
Let us walk by the sea, and watch the waves,
And see the fish gleam through the waters clear;
And I have tales to tell you of the past, —
The days when fairies hunted in the grass
On chargers small as are the gold-green flies
That star the air with fire; or of the days
When knights clad all in steel set thick with gold
Traversed the land to break enchanters' spells,
And free the long-haired damsels kept in chains
And held in noisome dungeons, where the light
Poured not its opulence of gifts; or days
When dryads shy lurked in the rustling woods,
And hooféd satyrs danced when old Pan played,

And through the roads of stars Diana sped,
The maiden-goddess white as are your thoughts,
My small Diana come to earth again.

ALFRED.

The stone just grazed him, we must turn and run,
Perchance he'd strike us with that slender stick;
I feel right grieved I did not hurt him sore,
But my hand trembled, and I could not throw.

IDA.

Now let us speed as quickly as we may;
I would not have you hurt him, but I fear,
And shall be glad to be at home again.

ALFRED.

Turn now and look — how his eyes follow us.

IDA.

How white he is, and seems most deeply sad;

If I but had more heart, I would go back,

And speak to him, and beg him not to mind,

And listen to one story, but I shiver so

I must get home; come, brother, hasten on.

V.

The Stranger.

I stand here trembling like a feeble boy,
As if the sweep of some experience,
Soul-shattering, and remoulding life in forms
That make the aspect of the universe
A face of deeper truth, had come upon me,
Had torn through all my body's space, and left
Me man quite alien to my former self.
My heart beats, and my breath comes quick and loud,
I seem to sigh, not breathe; it is all vain;
I dare not enter those forbidden haunts
Where general man builds homes, plies myriad tasks,
Plays games with vary-colored loves, seeks ends
Of transient glow, and on the fitful breaths
Of friends erects frail dwellings mutable.
I am so lightly swung on tenuous nerves,
That a faint wind that lifts no gossamer

In land of most men's lives, shakes me with shock

Of earthquake, and makes me to harbor fear

Lest my demesne in earth's firm-poised extent

Shall fall to dust, and past the reach of things

Be cast to realm of nothingness, and fall

Within annihilation's grasp. I fear

The converse where swift wit is masterful,

I tremble when I see the gathering crowd

Prepare to darken day with their weak speech,

Not fear, lest their base acts can work me harm,

Or futile thoughts bemire my statued calm,

But natural shrinking from their lower mind,

And innate horror of the stagnant pools

Wherein they dwell of thought and slavish hope;

Wherefore I needs must pause; how if I bind

These freest limbs with hateful bondages,

Break the blue-skied and sweet-aired leisure's calm

Under whose roof I pass mild days with clouds

Strange loves and curious hates shall quickly frame —

For these two are yoke fellows, never one

Appears unless the other walks full near.

If she would give up all her simple past,

Leave all behind what made her life before,

Wash from her memory what but brings it pain,

That on the white expanse of her large soul

I might write splendid thoughts of Heaven and God,

Bring her where shine the bright and changeless stars,

That in her lucid eyes their shapes might dwell,

That in her lucid mind the fiery spiritual sun

Of high philosophy might rise and burn,

And she would dwell in domes not built of hands,

But every stone a thought miraculous,

Each window a clear glass to deepest truth,

Each chamber some great dream of poet-sage,

Each door give access to the unsearched fields

Where bloom the eternal flowers that God still frames

Lest man his creature make an end of things,

And Niobe-wise proclaim his larger scope,

And dare rail at the Gods.   I tread the verge;

It may not be — the outer clamor sounds —

It may not be; the brother is a storm

Whose wrath makes dark the time I dream upon,

And in the mother's eyes no doubt are tears —

It may not be; for I cannot evoke

From slumber in a mother's deepmost heart

Sorrow and longing and their myriad tribes.

Pain is but of the world; and I would not

Stain my cleansed hands with implements of woe;

Even to think thereon makes my heart beat,

And the unuséd tears to flow; I feel

That at this price I purchased noble peace —

The world and its most clamorous dignities,

Its golden pomps, its strong ambition's steeps,

Its whirlwinds of applause that seize the soul

And bear it to a realm of passioned joy,

Its friendships that have something sweet and good,

Its love that builds an isle of maddest bliss,

Mingling the soul and frame in keen delight

Of frozen fire, as if the summer's heat

Should mix, a miracle, with winter's chill,

And from their strong embrace leaped forth a son

That joined their several joys — all these — all these —

I threw away as of small price or cost

That I might have ideal calm, the peace
Which is akin to God's, wherein swift dreams
Pursue great thoughts, and I am still at one
With the deep life that is in all that is.
Nay — I give her up; to breed great woe
In a dear mother's heart, a little one
To bear from the fireside where smiles and talk
Illumine more than the quick-leaping flames,
And ere the lights are set the shadows' play
Is weird and mutable as fancy's games
In children's hearts, is too hard task for me.
I consecrate anew life's brief remains
To clearest meditation, and those thoughts
That hold the universe in scope, to hopes
That lift humanity aloft to heights
Where the faint noise of struggle, grief, and pain
Shall change to music as things over-lived;
For in the memory's twilight, one by one,
The stars of long-done deeds arise, and grief
Outworn flames with a steady silver fire,
Till the vast night of the unforgotten past

Engirds with solemn splendor. I consecrate,

I consecrate, O God, me to thy service;

She is most fair, and I would fain see glow

The fire of grandest truths in her pure eyes;

But all this may not be, and I return

To my used solitude; to silent books

Wherein I pour my soul, and re-create

The minds majestic that upbore the world,

The imperial intellects that swerved time's course,

The living wills that were the seeds of acts

That shall not end save with the end of things.

4

VI.

IDA.

Ah, let us rest awhile ; I can no more,
And we are surely past his reach.

ALFRED.

                              You shake,
And you are white, and though you do not weep,
Your eyes seem as of one whose tears must flow.

IDA.

I cannot weep although I would ; I feel
Quite strange ; was there such cause for us to fear?

ALFRED.

I do not think it ; I had stood my ground,
But 'twas through you I acted as if need were
To fight him off ; now that I think on it,

You were quite foolish as you often are,

And with you near I do beyond my will

Things I should not attempt alone.

IDA.

O brother,

You must not talk so; ah, I weep at last;

Yet you are right as I so frequent find you.

My heart is sad when I fall on to think

How my weak fears broke in on several joys;

How white he seemed, and his voice shook alway

As if to speak were hard; if we had gone

Along the shore, and heard him tell his tales,

It had been better; yet I cannot tell

How some great dread took hold of me; I think

If he should come again, I'd do again

What now I grieve at, having done.

ALFRED.

Well — well —

It matters not, sweet sister, let us on.

IDA.

We are not far from home; we need not run,
And when we gain the path that rounds the hill,
We'll see the house, and mother at the door.

ALFRED.

See, sister, how the grass is full of blooms,
Low-drooping violets, and the snap-dragon,
And pale pink flowers I know not how to name.

IDA.

We can rest here awhile; you do not deem
That he will follow — ah, I am afraid.

ALFRED.

Here is a smooth white stone, where you can sit,
And the thick-leavéd tree makes pleasant shade.
He will not come, and we are so near home
That they would know our cries if trouble rose.

EXILE.

IDA.

'Tis so, indeed, and while we rest us here,

You can cull perfect flowers, and clover leaves,

And the long grass with delicate-woven top,

And I will bind them in a sweet bouquet

For mother; for you bear in mind she said

How wild flowers made her dream of happy days,

And seemed more tender than the flowers of home,

That made your heart beat, but these gentle blooms

Brought back the times when she was young like you

And full of glee.

ALFRED.

It is a happy thought;

Meanwhile you can recover from your scare,

And need not frighten mother with a tale

Of terrible nothing, for he meant no harm,

And when I see him, I will speak to him,

And ask him of the pictures and the book.

IDA.

I shall not easily forget my fear.
But here is your bouquet, the flowers well set
In a green border, and the spires of grass
In feathery tufts o'erhanging with thin shades
The pallid colors under.　Let us on.

ALFRED.

We reach the turn of road, and mother stands
Looking down the tree-bordered length for us.
She answers my quick wave of hat — come run.

IDA.

Nay, I must walk; I am all tired and hot,
And now I am to tell, my cheeks burn red,
And my strange fear renews.

ALFRED.

　　　　　　　　　　You need not speak;

I will relate the startling thing for you,

As you do always make the little great,

And out of a slim trifle weave a tale

That frightens mother, makes her white.

IDA.

No, no,

You cannot tell, for I have more to say

Than you know of.

MOTHER.

You have been very long.

Three times or more I stood at door to gaze,

And marvelled what detained my little ones.

But you remembered me — thanks for the flowers.

They have a freshness and a loveliness

More pure, more virginal, more subtly shy,

Than the unblushing city flowers that bare

Coquette-like their fierce beauty to the eye,

And challenge admiration all the time.

IDA.

Oh, dear mamma!

MOTHER.

What ails my little girl?
Have you been running, for you seem quite tired,
And shake as if much effort had unnerved,
Or set you trembling like a slender branch
A bird has leaped from?

ALFRED.

Let me tell the tale;
I shall not take so long, for going straight
I reach the end far quicker.

IDA.

Oh, mamma,
I am not tired, but he so frightened me,
That I must weep; and yet I feel sore shame;
For he was kind, and meant no harm; I spoiled
His wished enjoyment, and kind brother's too.

MOTHER.

Nay, child, you need not weep; I kiss your forehead,

And in my arms fear may not find a place.

My little one, come, ease yourself, be calm;

So, lay your cheek against mine; tell me now

Who *he* may be, and what adventure strange

Stirred in your heart such fear.

IDA.

I am ashamed;

He was right good, and brother wished to stay.

ALFRED.

You need not speak; we met the black-clothed man,

I told you how he gazed two days ago.

He came while we were both absorbed in play,

Looked on awhile with large surprisèd eyes,

Then praised my houses, spoke of picture books,

But sister felt such fear we ran away.

IDA.

There is much more; he spoke of his far home,

And all the splendors it enshrined, and asked,
Would I not go with him?   It is most strange,
But I felt quite as though I must obey,
I tremble now to think of it.

MOTHER.

Nay, child,

He spoke but as one might in jest, no doubt;
You cannot think he meant it otherwise.
Remember how but just a day ago
The lady you love so used the same words,
And you laughed as you clung to me.

ALFRED.

But I,

Dear mother, threw a stone at him that hit;
I do not deem it hurt — would that it had!

IDA.

You are too rude by far.

MOTHER.

Well, dry your eyes,
And we'll forget it all. You are at home,
And you shall go no more along the beach,
Save I or father may companion you.
And yet my little girl must cease these fears,
And bear a stouter heart.

FATHER.

Delay not more,
Go in, the dinner waits the truants twain.

ALFRED.

Father, was I far wrong because I threw?

FATHER.

We will not talk about it further now;
Go'in, and at more leisure we'll converse,
And penetrate the matter through and through,
Although remember still to play the part

Of a courageous brother apt to help. —

What shall be done with our sweet sensitive plant

That shuts when the breeze freshens? She was not made

For earth, but some ideal virginal realm,

Some land of solid dream, whose air is song.

Perchance she came from thence to light our home,

As a white lily lights the forest's gloom,

Or through a rent of cloud a mild star shines,

And saves the night from storm. Alas for us,

If we have not the power of wisest love

To bind her to us here.

MOTHER.

         Speak not such thoughts;

They clothe a real fear in garb fantastic,

A fear I shrink to put in words or form.

I drive it to some far recess of mind,

And lull it with the melodies of hope,

Till it falls on light sleep. I cannot think

Of aught befalling our most gentle child

Save life's divinest ministerings.

FATHER.

Forgive

If I have roused the woe you sang asleep.

I would that life withheld not high success,

That ever flies my best-adjusted aim.

For her dear sake I would have liberal wealth,

And that fine grasp of possibilities

That should assure to sight her lightest wish;

For she is fashioned in so noble mould

That no result of pride or baneful scorn

Could yet ensue upon her gaining all

That widest life can give.

MOTHER.

The same sad chord;

I bid you now again renounce the strain.

She will have love to wait upon her steps,

And make the frowning face of time relax,

And change to smiles; surely that is enough.

In your strong hands and gentle as great strength's,

She will be safe, and grow a human flower,

To make the space she dwells in full of joy.

FATHER.

If it prove so, it will not be to me
The high result is due.   A sudden thought;
'Tis he, indeed.

MOTHER.

                    You reproduce the child
In obscure hints of *he*.   Whom speak you of?

FATHER.

You know the sad recluse, the scholar mild,
Who dwells in outskirts of our busy town,
I saw him yestermorn in reverie
Pacing the beach, and wrapt in mystic dreams,
Scarce like a denizen of our world.

MOTHER.

                              I catch your sense.
I do not wonder at the child's affright;
His cold calm eyes, and utter-abstract mien,

Fill me with dread when at rare times I go
Past the great garden which the summer makes
A gem miraculous set upon the ring
Of our dear town.

FATHER.

I cannot longer doubt,
He is the man, and we must have great care
Of our dear girl's play on the beach; her frame
Can bear but ill these gusts of feeling strong
That are beyond the wont of her bright youth.

VII.

THE STRANGER.

Here let me rest; no shore is now in sight
Save as on either side a faint blue line.
No boat save mine pursued by the white foam
Cleaves the gray waters; I will ship my oars,
And let the boat drift with the wind and current.
The silence is so deep that I can hear
As 'twere the sound of time as it fleets by,
The flow of that unseen and mightier ocean,
Whereon the barks of states and lives and times
Have been borne forth to death or sure decay.
Beneath its voiceless waves the wrecks are hid
Of hopes that oversoared its blue of sky,
And stood at gaze on God; of joys that crushed
The whole world as clear grapes upon the lip,
And drank intoxication of red wine
That made the soul large as the universe

Scorn the earth's round as a child's outgrown toy;

Of fierce disdain upon whose lofty ridge

Stood poised the soul in utter rectitude,

And showed the world where Right shone as a sun.

Upon this dizzy verge the Present stands;

I look adown the abyss, and see the whirl

Of the fast-vanishing Past, and mightiest thrones

Of noblest virtues, images of dreams

Supernal, and extremest heights of thought,

Flicker like stars across that nether sky,

Burn, bicker, flash, are seen no more forever;

And like a mist wherein the strong winds strive

The Future rolls before, and underfoot

Solidifies, while all that is, is not,

Down-sunken in the gulf that waits for all.

O soul, that holdest in thy reach of thought,

Time with its vast contents, and teeming space,

Thou needst not tremble while the spectacle

Furls and unfurls, appears, appeareth not, —

The immutable mutation, changeless change,

That in its variability hath rest.

Is there no permanent? no higher thought
Wherein the riddle answers its own quest?
Nay, here are visions born of corporal eye,
Fair shapes the senses build and break, a world
That is but as the gazer looks upon 't.
Eternity is that concentring point
Wherein all rays of being merge, the Now
Born of the Past, and holding the To-Come
As seed for ripening; there, O soul, dwell thou;
Nay, dwell not, rather be thou that great thought,
That thou mayst grow the circling Universe,
That thou mayst flood all things with thine own self,
That thou mayst win true immortality.
The light breaks through the clouds with this deep thought,
As though the outer symboled in great joy
The rapture of discovery; 'tis well;
As on my soul floods the wide light of truth,
So flood, O sun, thy realm with radiancy.
It is a fair new day; I call it fair,
Although the somber gray of possible rain
Pervades the air, and the impetuous sun

Is shorn of half his glory or ere it falls.

Look to the hollow globe of sky — how fair!

In mass on mass of softest pearly tint,

And narrowing circles to the central point,

The mountainous clouds climb the steep curve of sky:

See there the space of unveiled central blue,

Intense in brightness past the power of words,

The fleece-like clouds in sweetly-broken shreds

Environing it; the waters lie below

A rippled floor of sober shine; ah me,

The wondrous air, most clear, most full of glow,

That every cloud and every fitful wave

Is dowered with perfect color; so I drift

Through the pale Paradise of simple Truth.

I mind me of the old philosopher

Who saw the pure Ideas in their dance,

Prefiguring the worlds, and, rapt in dreams,

Beheld the plains whereon the assembled souls

Choose lives to languish through beneath the moon.

Ah, can it be that on the upper air,

As on the ocean's waves, green shores advance,

And beings dwell whose drink is some fine ether,

Who scorn our gross embodiment, the garb

Wherein our souls are prisoned, and who are

Companions for the often-visiting Gods?

I poise me on yon cloud and dare to dream

How life is shaped in that cool placid realm,

A life of thought, clear, passionless, remote,

Unvexed by winds of fierce emotion, calm,

And resolute to pierce the core of things,

Bathed in the nearer sunlight, unbestained

With exhalations of our atmosphere.

But lo! I dream in sooth; not of the cloud

Is the pure vigor that has rapt my thought,

Not based on mists that from earth's ocean come,

And are but outwalls of its sullen realm;

Above the height of air and concave sky,

That limits mind of terrene men, I soar

Into the thinner ether, which to breathe

Slays the dull body's weight, and robes the soul

In nudity of clear expression, form

That is Idea's self; but see, I drift

Close to the shore, and the sun's burnished rays

Clothe with light fierce as many-flashing steel

A single spot in the encincturing landscape,

All else being wrapped in shadow pale, subdued;

Like gems the sweetly-shapen trees drink in

And then reflect the partial splendor; a path

Winds through the gold-green arch of greeting trees,

And at the avenue's end a white small house,

And children at their play. It cannot be!

And yet the thrill of pleasure that unmans me

Cannot deceive! That purpose will not down!

Ah, now I hear her laugh; it is the voice,

And as she moves, I see the childish grace

That has a charm such as a queen of elves

Might hold her subjects with; I do not err.

She penetrates by mystic accident

My solitude wherein I hoped to tear

My roots of life out from the alien soil

They deeply clung to, dreams where she was queen.

Yet must I be a slave to whim and hope,

Be fettered by desire for earthly good,

Care for some waif of rude humanity,

Be tossed at will on waves of bitter love?

But I must think aright; the experiment

Is worth endeavor; I should make the girl

The pearl, the crown of womanhood; all Time

Her hand should wear as some slight ornament

That emphasizes beauty; secret lore

From the unfathomed Orient's store, and grasp

Of Nature that makes her obey the will,

With those high truths the sages hid in myth

Lest the profane should read, I'd give for dower;

I may not yield; I will resume the search,

And bear my bird unto my eager hearth,

Not for that she shall dwell there sad and caged,

But that her song, grown strong with justest use,

(The bounds of her sweet home being overpassed,

And youth's much need of wisdom's guidance done)

Shall fill the reaches of the world's wide wood

With more than native fire of song, and rapture

Wherein the soul finds her primeval peace.

Ah ha! a fury seizes me, a joy

That has not torn me since my vanished youth,

Since the fierce days when in the whirl of life

I plunged as a strong swimmer in the waves

Whose reckless foam burns gold in the high sun.

I swiftly seek the shore, I cannot fail,

It is a work set for me by the years.

Unto this height I clomb from whence all things

Are but slight elements in the vast view,

The oversight that merges in a point

The multitudinous universe, that has

The All engrasped, of knowledge absolute

The peak and summit; hither my soul has flown,

That it might ope the doors of some deep mind,

Might pierce the darkness of intelligence

That glooms it round, and, having shown the truth,

Arm it for fight with men — my task, indeed,

Save for my feeble flesh, and halting breath —

And so my world-work will be well fulfilled.

My little prophetess, your melodies

Will pierce the slumberous ears of the old world,

Awake the time to knowledge of high truth,

Give wings to cruel-fettered Liberty;

For I shall die, but thou wilt be my soul,

To shed my thoughts as leaves upon the winds,

As rays of light upon the air, or rain

From highest clouds upon the thirsty fields,

My little singer, whose deep thought am I!

VIII.

IDA.

Ah, do not stir; we'll watch the brown small bird
That stands here in the grass; note his clear eye,
And how he moves his lissome neck; ah, now
He flits upon the tree's swayed branch, and gazes;
There, he is gone, a brown speck in the air,
Cleaving his way as the slim fish the sea.

ALFRED.

Father, when shall we go down in the town?
Is it your wish to have the boat made ready?

FATHER.

It is not time; I wish to stay awhile,
My book has yet some pages to be read,
And I am here so pleased with the cool peace
That I shall hardly care to go.

ALFRED.

Well, then,

May I go out alone?

MOTHER.

Nay, be content,

And sister soon shall go with you.

ALFRED.

I'm tired;

You all have books, or Ida watches birds,

Or, stretched upon the grass, looks at the flowers.

I know not whither I may turn.

IDA.

Dear brother,

Look up into the sky. High overhead

The thick clouds seem asleep, but under them

Thin films, most white and pure, float on the wind,

And where the sunlight falls, they softly shine,

As if all through them flashed a sudden joy,
And they are lighted as a face with smiles.

ALFRED.

It is a pretty sight; the large clouds break,
And the thin shreds float on, showing the sky's
Pale blue through their faint woof.

IDA.

We'll play;
The little clouds shall be our messengers,
We'll give them thoughts to bear, what do you think?

ALFRED.

A silly game; but as I needs must stay,
'Twill do to pass the time.

MOTHER.

Nay, that is sullen;
Besides the day grows hot, and on the water

The strong sun beats unhindered, save for the shades
The swift clouds throw.

ALFRED.

But in the boat 'tis cool :
For the large wind has play, and calms the heat.

IDA.

On with our game.   I see a slender waif
Float on the wind as a white fairy skiff;
I bid it bear for me a beam of light
To fall upon a lady's finger ring,
And call from sleep the fire and gold are there.

ALFRED.

I give that large white bark with back-blown pennon
A wind to hold, whence it shall flutter loose
Against the small sail glittering far away,
That the swayed boat may skim the yielding waves
With speed to make one glad.

IDA.

Mamma, you speak;
You send the dearest wishes, and 'tis joy
To have you mix with us in play.

MOTHER.

I send
Upon that highest cloud a golden dream,
A dream that may come true, a dream of love,
That melts in bright reality — for whom?
For the pale stranger that you met and feared.

ALFRED.

Now, father, 'tis your turn.

FATHER.

If I shall play,
I send upon that swiftest cloud a Thought,
A Truth, that it may poise above the head
Of the pale student, flash through his tossed brain,

Lighting the white transparent face with flame,

And making clear the mystery he pursued

For weary years with swift discovery.

ALFRED.

I see afar a cloud with wings outspread

Quite like a bird; I hang upon its neck,

My carrier-pigeon's neck, an unseen missive,

That all the boys may learn of the wide world,

How glad it is to feel the wind and spray

Dash on your face when out far on the sea.

IDA.

I see a cloud all fervent with the sun,

Washed with the light, and sailing slow afar;

Into that downy nest I set a bird,

The bird of a sweet song, that will be borne

Back to our home, and there abide for us,

Till in the winter time it melts in tone,

And our rapt thoughts are carried back again

To this sweet shore, to this faint-sounding sea,

To the fair rose-glen just beyond the house,

To those bright flakes of fire upon the deep.

ALFRED.

Upon that great white ball I place a statue,

King-like and crowned; let him compel the nations

To hold our land in reverence.

IDA.

On the verge,

Where the horizon gray curves to the sea,

A thinnest vapor speeds; 'tis scarce a cloud,

And more like light slow-hardening; in its woof

I mix I know not what, a drop of soul,

That out of it a rain may fall on hearts

Fulfilled of pain, and they may quickly wake

As from a dream, and be mild-glad again.

ALFRED.

I have enough; father, read us a tale,

From the old book you were so glad to find,
And much surprised with yesterday, of how
The king went hunting through the enchanted wood,
And found his lady changed into a vine.

MOTHER.

A happy thought; we all are just in mood
To hear; and those rich oriental plays
Need to be read when we, in tune with nature,
Feel not abrupt the change from daily mind
To that sublimed and mystic consciousness.

IDA.

I sit upon the grass next to mamma;
It is as well as going in the boat.

ALFRED.

'Twill do awhile; but I prefer to row,
And fight the wind, and cut right through the wave,
And know how strong I am.

FATHER.

I have the place;
Shall I go o'er the part we read last time?

MOTHER.

A pleasant thought; but lo! a stranger stands
At the path's turn, and is at point to come.

IDA.

Let me go in the house; for it is he,
And I yet fear to meet him.

ALFRED.

What foolishness!
You said you would be braver, and you blench
The first time you are tried; I mean to stay
And hear him speak.

FATHER.

Nay, children, get you in,

6

Or play in the green field behind the house;
We shall remain to build acquaintanceship.

IDA.

Come, brother, like a dear good boy; ah me,
I tremble when I see him.   I will play
The least game that you like, come but with me.

THE STRANGER.

Your pardon if my suddenness offend,
And yet I deemed a fellow-townsman's right   ·
Would fail not recognition.

MOTHER.

                      You are welcome,
Pray you be seated; it is a pleasant thing
To meet away from home co-dwellers there;
It gives a sense of shattered lonesomeness,
And strips the place of strangeness.

THE STRANGER.

                            Yet strangeness surely

Can have slight hold where friendship pitches tent,
And family cheer sets up abiding place.

FATHER.

True, sir; we bid you be that cheer's partaker,
And it will give us joy if we have power
To make you feel at home, so be there's need.

THE STRANGER.

You make me welcome to far better home,
I deem, than the outer can build up; in books,
Where greatest minds have reared an unseen world,
That is unto the things we see as soul,
A nobler dwelling is, more permanent,
More native to our best capacities.

FATHER.

Into that realm you will be worthy guide;
Report that lives on lips of wisest men
Holds little error, and we know to you

That realm's each flower-lit glade, each greenest nook
Of ancient wood, its smooth white sands of shore,
Stray slopes of blossom-joy in mountain folds,
High table-lands that rule the unmeasured fields,
All places of deep thought, and those hid founts
Of feeling where to drink opes the soul's eyes
To occultest mysteries, are as good friends:
We shall have joy to tread upon your steps.

The Stranger.

Nay, sir, repute still speaks with too large sound;
For through the yielding air the spoke word spreads,
And reaches ear with loud reverberation,
As a weak king enpanoplied in gold,
And wearing reflex glow of retinue,
May seem a very Cæsar.

Mother.

But the clear page
Whose magic letters hide a visible truth,
And are of might to fuse an alien soul

In noblest gladuess, speaks more loud than fame
The sentences the latter utters.

THE STRANGER.

Be it so :
I dare belie not the deep work of years ;
For I have trodden many paths of thought,
Pursued to their far haunts evanishing truths,
Found ways to disentangle thinnest woofs
Of the arch-worker, spirit, gazed upon
The elements wherefrom his world is made,
And watched him at his labors till I knew
Some deepest secrets of his handicraft,
And took his tools, and furthered his results.
But 'tis not of myself I mean to speak,
Forgive the self-love of a lonely man,
Who joins too little converse with his kind
To mould his speech to their accredited fashion.

MOTHER.

Dear sir, it is our valued privilege,
To step aside from the accustomed ways,

And with great sages meditate the world,
Not in its semblance, marvellous deceit,
But as it is to the opened eye of soul,
That visions not this realm of sense and time,
But the essential whole which is the life,
And in whose self-recurrent pulse all things,
All times, all histories, all human thoughts,
Are points of fact wherefrom it ever builds
Its mighty fabric — nay, I speak but ill,
Not it, but He who is the Life of Life,
And Soul of Soul.

FATHER.

Go not into those depths;
The young day laughs, the gray clouds break away,
The sun points to the sea, a wealth of smiles,
And gives command with sweetest tyranny
To be like it, our wondrous molten souls
To break in luminous ripples of fleet joys,
And ever-changing gleams of lightsomeness.

THE STRANGER.

A trip in yonder boat were not amiss;

Out to the central bay, afar from land,

In places where the many rarely come,

And the wide loneliness of sea and sky

Engulfs you in its clearness; underneath

The fluent waters, overhead the viewless air,

Away from all solidity, the soul —

A joy past earthly words to subtly frame —

Convinced of its eternity, and freed,

Or glad-forgetful of its body chains,

The world and all that is a fixed mere point,

Whereon it bird-like is light-poised awhile.

MOTHER.

Your words bring to my mind the poet's words —

His of the fiery soul, whose home was air,

And whose deep heart was torn with this world's woes,

That reddened his fierce song's absolving flow;

You know the verses well: "I love all waste

And solitary places, where we taste

The pleasure of believing what we see

Is boundless as we wish our souls to be."

FATHER.

That poet seems a favorite; strange to me,
For he is mainly read and loved of men.

THE STRANGER.

But in the realm of mind all severance dies,
There oneness dwells, no barren monotone,
But unit-life ensphering all diverse.
Surely in thought the man or woman dies,
And simple human re-asserts itself.

FATHER.

I cry you mercy — for the noble day
Still bids me bathe in its circumfluous sea;
I would but breathe and be, so wonderful
The golden clearness governs me.

MOTHER.

       I, sir,
Would give you thanks; I care not overmuch
For those diversities our crude life frames,

And dwell by preference on those subtle hints

Of inner calm in whose mild atmosphere

All storms absorbed as 'twere into the sun

Yield place to grander forces.

THE STRANGER.

Hark! a laugh

Rings clear against the air — your child's, I doubt.

FATHER.

Our little girl's whom you perchance have seen.

THE STRANGER.

I met two children playing in the sand,

A strong, stout boy, of a courageous mien,

And masculine eye, that dared the total world,

Companioned by a golden-haired sweet girl,

On whose pure face pure dreams had left their glow,

In whose wide eyes sat an unspotted soul,

Looking in strangeness on this lower realm,

As troubled with some unacquaintanceship,

And yet at point to dower it with its love.

MOTHER.

Our children build a world within the world,

And we together are a spiritual isle,

Engirt by the wide sea of all mankind,

An individual happiness, indeed,

But drawing life from the universal soil.

THE STRANGER.

No doubt you have the secret; I have sought,

But cannot say, have found; I feel the feud;

In solitude the shapes of grandest thoughts

Float in pure light before mine inner eyes;

But on the rapture of high meditation

There supervenes a mighty loneliness;

And yet the world of men I shudder from,

And know not how to bear myself in it.

FATHER.

Perchance, love holds the key; forget oneself,

Bind life with other lives, and the wide sky

Is clear of clouds.

THE STRANGER.

I deem your words are true;
I would bestow my wealth's large sovereignties
On others; the power I grasp, so vast, so strong,
I am not apt to wield; no doubt young hands,
Made strong by will suffused of truest thought,
Might take the full nihility of wealth,
And bare the eternal statue lurking there.

MOTHER.

What better use of wealth than personal grace
Wrought in the soul by studious hold of books,
And making beautiful the transient spot
Wherein we dwell? Think you not so with me?

THE STRANGER.

Experience answers nay. I would have one —
A child — a soul unharmed with life as yet —
To whom might fall the dower of perfect freedom;
She should have space to grow as grows a flower,
Fed by each wind full-freighted with God's stores,

Bathed in the light of his unceasing suns,

Taking from earth the best it has to give.

It were a task to soothe the approach of age,

And rob grim death of terror. I should live

In my sweet pupil.

FATHER.

For you not hard to find,

I deem.

MOTHER.

A pure desire well worth success.

THE STRANGER.

You have a child — a lovely golden girl —

And I — I might confer great benefits on her;

I am alone — I have not friends — but much —

Much else you know of — you are townsman mine.

FATHER.

Nay, sir, your words are hard to understand.

You cannot mean —

MOTHER.

You speak of our bright girl?
You would have her? take her from mother's side?
I cannot listen longer — let me go.

FATHER.

Sweet wife, be calm; here is some mystery;
I am not clear in what is said nor you;
Explain yourself, kind sir, for we would hear.

THE STRANGER.

Forgive — I cannot now — I will return.
I am so little used to converse — I will go —
Consider you my words — it will be best.
She shall be queen — nor of the world alone —
But reign in the white land of intellect,
A sovereign woman, marvel of her times,
A light to burn adown the dusky road
Along which move the ages newly risen,
A fire to enflame in all men's hearts to come
Fierce love of truth, and all that is the best,

Another virgin giving to these sad latter times

A spiritual birth of deepest thought and hope,

In whose unceasing current whoso bathes,

Shall be reborn in inmost soul — but lo!

I speak wild words, yet not words void of truth.

Forgive — bethink you well — it will be best.

I shall return.

MOTHER.

He is not right in mind;

I feel as I should weep — for him — for me —

I know not well.   What meant his passioned words?

Tear from my side my little loving girl,

Who needs a mother's hand, a mother's heart,

Whose soul would flutter in his gilded cage

As some bird newly caught, pining for wood

And cool up-bearing winds?   I am not clear

I seize his sense.

FATHER.

Take peace unto yourself;

He has lived long alone, and knows not well

How men are linked together, hence his strangeness.

Pity for him I beg who has torn his roots

Out from the general soil, and so must bear

An alien's part within the unheeding world.

IX.

The Stranger.

Shall I succeed?   The doubt obtrudes itself;
I have been wrong, and clearly see wherein.
Thought is not solitary, rather grows
From contact of all souls; you break the charm,
And enter Fancy's changeful realm who hope
From thought's mere exercise to build up truth.
My little girl shall be an avenue,
A flower-fringed way to lead my footsteps back;
I hear her laugh sound through my vacant rooms,
And the large house recovers life and soul,
Touched by her magic finger; as in the tale,
A myriad hopes and possibilities,
And many fair delights have fallen on sleep
In the wide kingdom of my heart; and she,
My princess, wakens all in this changed version
Of fairy-lore remote.   I cast off fear,

I throw aside the cold reserve of years,

I mix with the deep life of human kind;

I know their joys, I feel the wondrous thrills

Of ecstasy that are their common fare,

I stand no more aloof; is it not true

That feeling holds the All dissolved as pearl

The Egyptian queen drank off in ruby wine?

I face the twin infinities; lo! Thought,

Amid whose placid plains and silver streams

These many years my constant feet have gone;

Lo! Bliss, a sea on which I dare to float.

I see the sister hold the brother's hand,

And melt division of the bodily frame

In one sweet innocent joy; I see the child

Stand by its mother's knee, and in their eyes

Their souls are one; I see friend walk with friend,

And the mild stream of converse is themselves,

No more dissevered, but each mixed with each;

The husband holds his wife against his breast,

And in the rapture of their beating hearts,

Fair marriage of two souls is consummate.

7

And lo! the world of passion; shall I quake,

And shudder back when these fierce gates expand?

The lover scatters kisses on his mistress' lips,

As in the wood, which a dim stillness holds,

The rose-leaves fall upon the moist soft grass;

Vague thrills of fear and hope assail his breath,

And in a dream he swoons, wherein his queen

Is mystic mistress of the winds and streams,

And nought is but themselves; and e'en the depths

Of mad delights, where still the soul is torn

By gusts of joy and hate, I dare explore;

The goddess of all lovers, pale and wan,

I see within her caverned mount, and him,

The knight who bartered life and hope for her,

Who chose sad love in lieu of God's own bliss.

But now an end, I must no longer rave;

I dare not trust that she will walk beside me,

And if I fail, I give up all attempt.

The trouble comes, I sacrifice the higher,

Pure intellect, to what is of the lower born

Perchance, and on that way is certain death.

Ah, wretched that I cannot cling to one,

But must bewilder me with many aims.

It is not done, they will refuse, I deem,

And I return to my unrippled calm:

That were the best, methinks; — what is the right?

Will they forego to see her, hear her, love her?

Have I the right to tear from mother's side

The child, and be a double criminal?

Criminal — harsh word, nor yet devoid of truth.

Down with these fears!   For once I am a man,

A doer in the endless whirl of things,

No passive looker-on: what comes shall come!

Meanwhile I put forth utmost power of hand

To grasp the fruit has pleased my eager sense.

I will give over thought, the balancing

Of many points of view, adjustment nice

Of motives filmy as the woven air,

Or quickly-vanishing mist, unravelling

Of elements fine as outspread web of light,

That garments the bright sky, a chemistry

Of spirit or of dream ; lo ! I will act

And bathe me in the stream of consequence,

Whereby I shall be man past what I've been,

Yea, be in truth the deed, the power of God!

X.

IDA.

But do you think he'll come again?

MOTHER.

I do.

IDA.

Then brother may go with me to the beach?

ALFRED.

Not so; I wish to stay, and hear him talk.

FATHER.

Yes, you shall stay; we shall not see him after,
And both shall hear the words he speaks.

IDA.

Dear mother,
Close by your side I shall not be afraid.

ALFRED.

What kind of man is he?

FATHER.

He is a scholar,
Has traversed many lands, and noted much,
Has studied deepest books and gathered lore
That none but loftiest intellects dare pursue.
He is most subtile, and I more than deem
Has lost himself amid a maze of thoughts,
So that no more he has a grasp of life,
But floats as a stray leaf upon the flood,
Or bubble through the many-pathèd air.

ALFRED.

You say what I can get no meaning from.

FATHER.

Most true; I lost your question, dearest boy,
And merely thought aloud: he's a wise man,
And yet I cannot call him good.

ALFRED.

He spoke
Of picture books, of churches, old and fair,
Of mansions wide and grand he meant to show me.

FATHER.

No doubt he might if so he felt inclined.

IDA.

But he is sad, and in my utmost fear
My heart weeps for him.

MOTHER.

There spoke my little girl;
He more excites our pity than our dread.

FATHER.

You know we have not wealth; how if he came,
And sought to bear you to his noble home,
And bring to pass your every lightest wish,
For he has power.

IDA.

I shake with sudden chill;
These words are not for me?

MOTHER.

I hold you fast;
It is a jest, a trifle cruel.

IDA.

Him?
Go forth with him, and leave you all behind?
Say, must I go?   But I shall surely die.
Dear brother, come to me; what can it be?
I soon shall tremble at you, father, —

ALFRED.

You shall not go so long as I am by;
They cannot tear you from me, so be still.

MOTHER.

Appease the child; you will forego her love,
And much I fear me 'twill be somewhat long
Or ere she loses memory of this shock.

FATHER.

Forgive, dear child; I cannot tell you why,

But somehow I felt bound to say the words.

You should be free, I would not force your choice,

Though filial love makes you our own. Enough;

You are too young to understand my purpose.

MOTHER.

Your words make me ashamed of my swift harshness.

But lo! the stranger comes.

THE STRANGER.

I have returned.

MOTHER.

We give you greeting, sir.

THE STRANGER.

I would be plain,

And to my business pass at once.

FATHER.

Business?

MOTHER.

Let him proceed.

THE STRANGER.

To you I'd speak, sweet child;
I am a lonely man, and your clear smile
Is as the moon to my dark life's sad night.
Nay, tremble not; I shall give you much love,
And you will speak but to achieve your will.

IDA.

I am most sorry for you.

THE STRANGER.

Ah, gladness comes
When you are near; you will not flee again?

IDA.

Your sadness grieves me, but I know you not.

ALFRED.

You brought the picture books you promised me?

THE STRANGER.

I do forget — and yet — not now — not now —
Hereafter I may send you them. Dear girl,
Stand by me here, and let me hold your hand.

IDA.

No — no — I would not leave my mother's side;
Here I am safe — and you — I know you not,
You are too strange.

FATHER.

You spoke of business, sir.

THE STRANGER.

I do recall myself; your pardon.
I shall mean no offence, but I would speak
With freedom, and make clear my long desire.

FATHER.

Speak without fear; it is my pleasure's wont,
I have no love for windings in and out.

THE STRANGER.

I have great wealth, this is no news to you;
I have small faith in that munificence
Which feeds its vanity by large bequests
To public charities; the donor's will
Is not expressible in perfect words,
And the keen law's interpretative skill
Brings manifold meanings from distinctest speech;
So the bequest is tortured from its end,
And waters fields quite alien from the hope.
I would bestow my gifts with lesser failure.

FATHER.

You well express my thought; to be dispenser
Of one's own bounties seems the wiser course.

THE STRANGER.

You pardon me, I would enrich you, sir,
And change the dull monotony of your days
To graceful interchange of pure delights,
And harnessing the courser, property,

To the swift car of your sweet family cheer,

Set you at freedom from material chains,

And leave the world to master as you wished.

FATHER.

Too large a gift, too slender toil for me;

Achievement is the best reward of work.

I should refuse the gift.

THE STRANGER.

Nay, hear me through;

I am a lonely man; I would find way

To sweet communion with my fellow-man.

The sense of glad society is long disused,

And of itself the blossom will not grow.

I must find other means, and with your help

I shall not fail in its resuscitation.

FATHER.

If I can serve you in so wise a wish,

'Twill give me joy.

THE STRANGER.

You have a fairy child, —
Her hand shall guide me from my wilderness,
Shall starwise lead me from the labyrinth,
As in the ancient days the enamored princess
Led the Athenian stranger to the light.

FATHER.

I pray you come at once to your sure point:
In this obscure of words no thought is clear,
And I must guess your purport.

THE STRANGER.

Nay, not guess:
We both shrink from the edge; then here it is.
This golden-haired fair child, this visible dream,
I would receive from you; I'll bear her hence,
A daughter mine. The world shall be her toy,
She shall be queen of the world's intellect,
Upon the waves of fame her name shall float,
A ship to bear great truths to sundered lands,

All womanhood centred in her noble life
Shall vaunt itself to have borne such prodigy,
Upon the mountain-peaks of time shall burn
Her beacon-thoughts to rouse the sluggish nations;
What would you more? you cannot say me nay.

FATHER.

You deem the answer easy; will the child
Return at intervals to home and friends?
For these, I doubt, in light of grandiose aims
Might fade as night's most fiercely splendent stars
Die on the breast of the effulgent sun.

THE STRANGER.

Return to home and friends? strange speech to make;
What have these here to do?

MOTHER.

Have you a heart?
You'd tear a soul from all it holds most dear,
Sever as with a knife bonds red with blood,

Make a young life as cold and lone as yours,

Suppress the love that flows 'twixt mother and child,

And then you say these have here naught to do?

FATHER.

Nay, wife, no more. My daughter, listen well;

You see this gentleman; he offers you

Wealth far beyond your wish — and I am poor —

All things that make life worth desire to live,

Fame, splendor, power to do mankind much service,

Far more than your young years can understand,

And I can give you but a dubious joy —

For I am poor — save that you will be girt

By purest love; now you are free to choose;

Will you go forth with him?

IDA.

                          I catch your sense;

O mother, loosen not your grasp from mine;

I have no more to say.

ALFRED.

I hate you, sir;
If you come here again I shall be wroth,
And take sure means to do you some fell harm.

FATHER.

You have our answer, sir.

THE STRANGER.

I hear not well;
This looks like a refusal — folly dire! —
Shall I not have the child?

MOTHER.

I can no more;
I pray you leave us now in peace.

THE STRANGER.

No — no —
I yet am at dull loss; my brain turns round;
You cannot be so cruel, yield the child.
A mother's selfishness should here give way.

8

FATHER.

Enough; you seem not swift to apprehend;

Have you not thought how in our close-meshed life

The law prevails of cost and price? Ah, sir,

Not fully-formed into our grasp is given

The thing we seek; out of hard sacrifice

As from some savage jaw 'tis ours to rend

What so we yet desire. You dare to ask

The sweetest gift of man, nor reck the cost?

Go! mix with men, dispense your charities,

In some fair woman's eyes no doubt you'll see

The image of your aims reflected clear;

Then out of duties nobly done, and work

Beside your fellows, as God's visible chrism,

There will descend from heaven your dear reward,

Your child, incarnate symbol of much toil,

And yielding up of self, your own, no fruit

Plucked from another's tree, and lacking taste

To soothe your hungered heart; you ask in vain

What we've not right to give, and, being given,

Could bring but death to you and her.

THE STRANGER.

And yet
My thought is pure; you break my latest hope;
To see my intent in mirror of your words
Is horrible. Can I be lost so far?
I am not used so to mistake the right,
Yet you seem right; I am quite broken down,
Grant me the time to gain my surer calm.

MOTHER.

Take comfort; we are sad to give you pain.

FATHER.

These are grave depths of thought; it is not well
To deem oneself sufficient unto all.
In this dark mystery that we call life
The appulse of souls and things and deeds so close
Connects the each with all that disarray
Means exile; as the tree draws life from air,
Yet rooted in the soil has dwelling-place,
And perishes withdrawn from vital circle,

So there survives no deed save as with all

It mixes in the spiritual ebb and flow

That is the soul of this vast universe;

Thought abstract feeds upon itself, a phantasm,

It traverses all time and space nor rests;

Life fills it with red blood, though yet I deem

Mere living is but brutishness and dirt;

In realm of pure Idea is the source

Of light, we walk in darkness otherwhere.

THE STRANGER.

The attempt is over. If I have given offence,

Forgive. I am recovered from disease;

There needed but this last experience

To render plain how that for men like me

The intellectual is the sole repose.

XI.

THE STRANGER.

I feel deep shame — I must regain my calm;
But I shall prove apt learner. Here is end;
True, I was wrong to hope acquaintanceship
With action's small dexterities a task
Requiring little time; the soul descends
With troubled steps into an alien region.
The wisdom offered me with free outpour
I long have found stale and unprofitable.
Men have their functions, and the thinker stern
Is not the least of creatures; but I feel shamed
At having touched that baser sphere, and known
Weak thrills of soft lascivious feeling stir
My heart bemired; some large and cleansing thought
Shall rid me of these stains! In the clear stream
Of some great book I needs must bathe, perform
Some vast and expiatory toil of brain.

I scorn myself, the humiliation beats

Against my brows, and drains my veins of blood.

The truths they spake have only relevance

Where souls yet infantile perforce seek aid

From mutual stress, that subtle slavery

Whence highest man superb erects himself,

And being all, is freedom, his true self.

But I shall soon forget; these latest throes

Fall from me as the cool clear drops of rain

From burnished leaves amid the sober wood.

I am given to myself once more — and never hence

Shall I make wandering; where I early found

The voice of passion fail in the far reaches,

And youth's hot tumult melt in grateful peace,

I shall abide; the wall of chill reserve

I build more just and firm. Here is no failure,

Rather a clear recall my inmost soul

Sounds, that no further I may tread the steep,

And fall to lot of common humankind.

Like one who travels from a city's bounds,

And sees the lessening lights upon the night,

And the wide circle of his sight grows lone,

But overhead the large-faced moon is calm,

And the great winds are free to utter speech —

The city's tumult left behind, the pain of friendship,

The fierce remorse of love, the belittling sense

That comes of too much intercourse with men,

All these and worser left behind forever —

While the vext heart resumes its nobler peace,

The sea of thought upheaves no more with storm,

And inner weds the outer large repose,

Like him who thus hath found what long he sought,

I wander inward from the wizard sense,

Release me from its many dear deceits,

And rest me in the spirit's solitude.

O mighty Thought!   O Silence vast, profound!

O region of Ideals still, majestic,

The very temple and the home of Gods,

The atmosphere of causes, and the eagle-nest

Of glorious influences ruling all the worlds,

In you my mind and soul shall ever dwell!

O noblest Truth! to you is dedicate

My mind, my strength, my hope, my all of being,

You take I for my bride, you sole I love,

Upon your altar as a sacrifice

I shed my blood, and sink in wordless rest!

THE END.